This book
belongs to

....

For Dad (aka Grandpa)

Tick-Tock
Copyright©2020 by Allison Parkinson
Published by Tiger's Eye Books
tigerseyebooks.co.uk
Cover and formatting: Vicki Bloomfield
First paperback print edition:
2020 in the United Kingdom

ISBN: 978-1-9161948-1-6

Tick-Tock

Written and illustrated
by Allison Parkinson

Grandpa's bought a creepy clock.

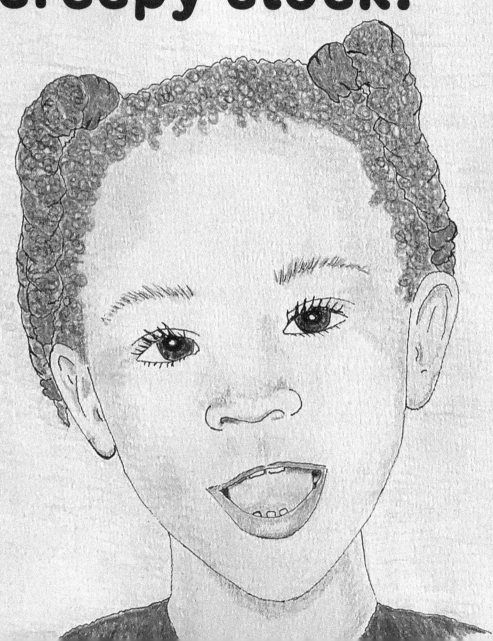

Tick-Tock, Tick-Tock

He found it in an antiques shop.

Tick-Tock, Tick-Tock

It's made of wood,
it's very old.

Tick-Tock, Tick-Tock

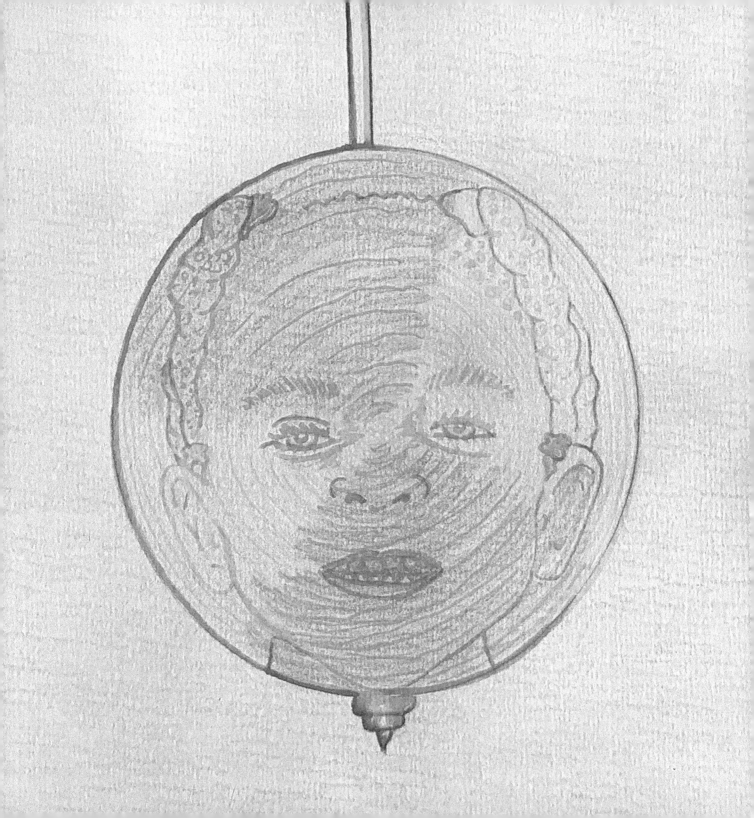

And has a pendulum that's gold.

Tick

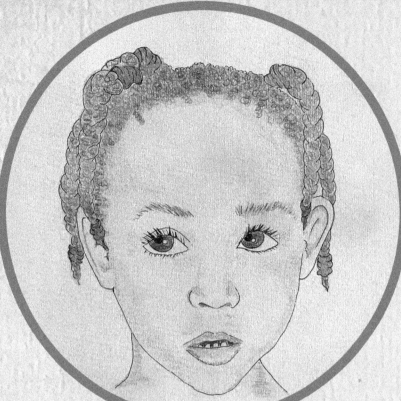

Tock

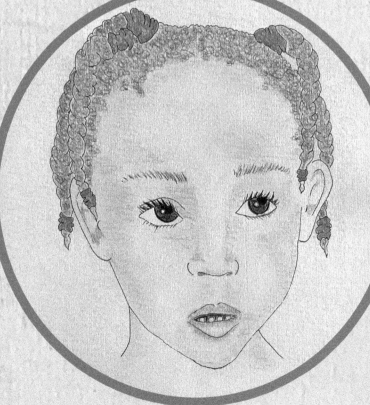

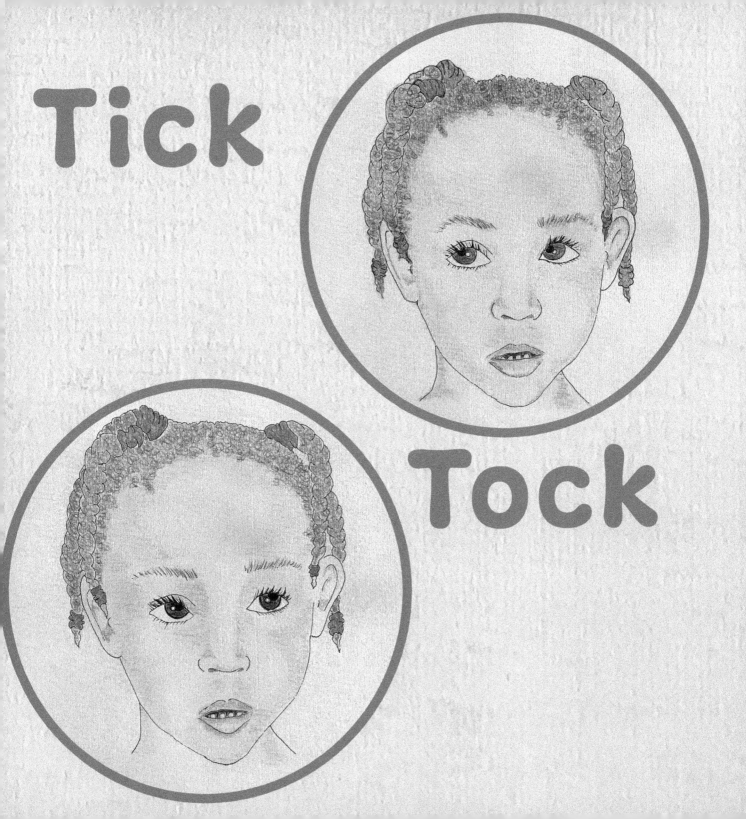

Tick

Tock

Its big round face is flat and white.

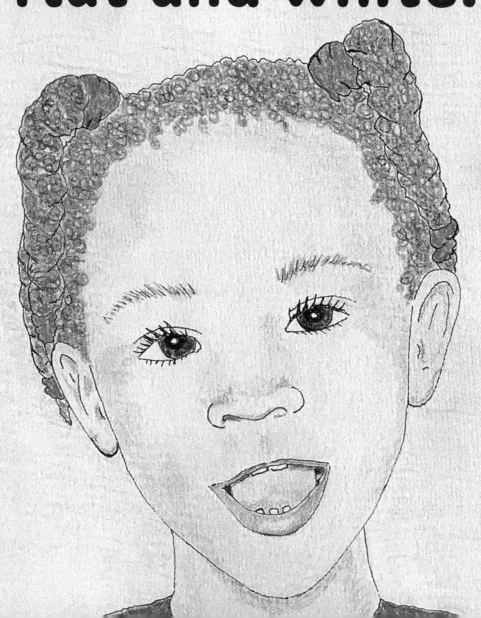

Tick-Tock, Tick-Tock

Which gleams like a full moon at night.

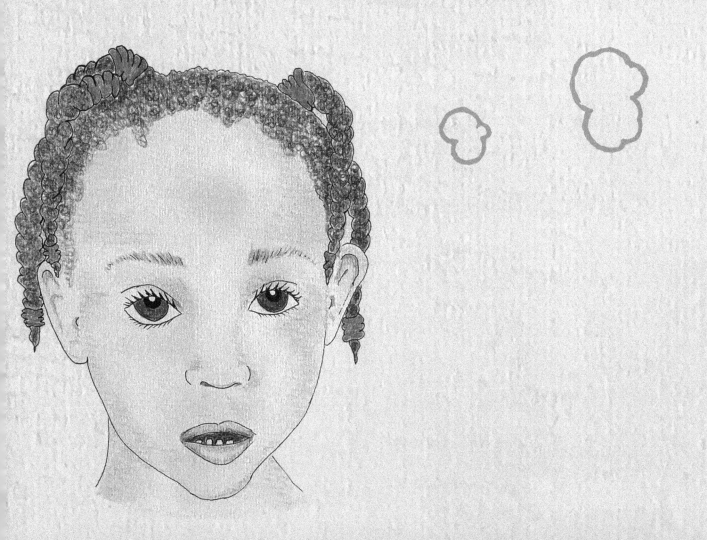

It has two hands: one big one small.

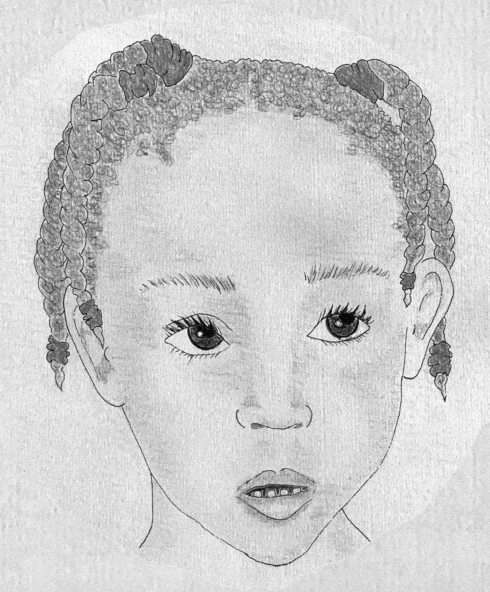

Tick-Tock, Tick-Tock

I don't like the clock at all.

Look!

A teeny, tiny door.

Tick-Tock, Tick-Tock

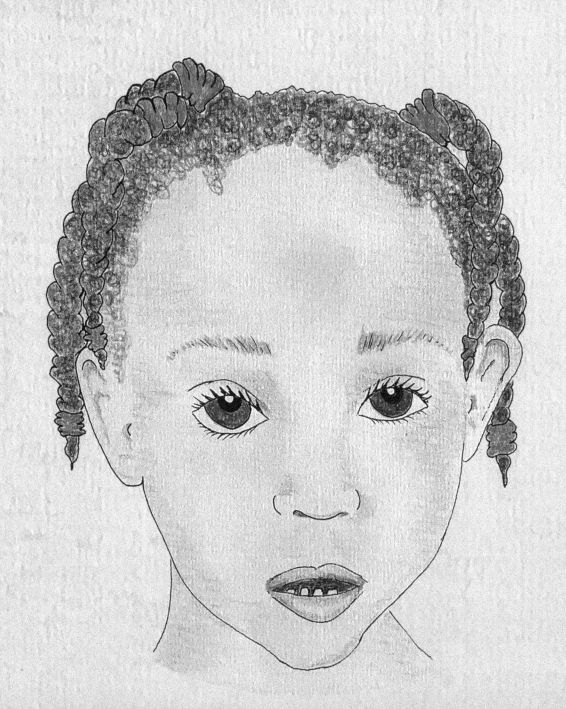

I haven't noticed that before.

Tick-Tock, Tick-Tock

I wonder what's behind that door.

Tick-Tock, Tick-Tock

I want to see...

but
I'm
not
sure.

Tick-Tock, Tick-Tock

Should I take a little peek?

Tick-Tock, Tick-Tock

Something in the clock went 'squeak'!

Tick-Tock, Tick-Tock

The little hand's jumped to the...

Tick-Tock,
Tick-Tock

Something clicked behind the door!

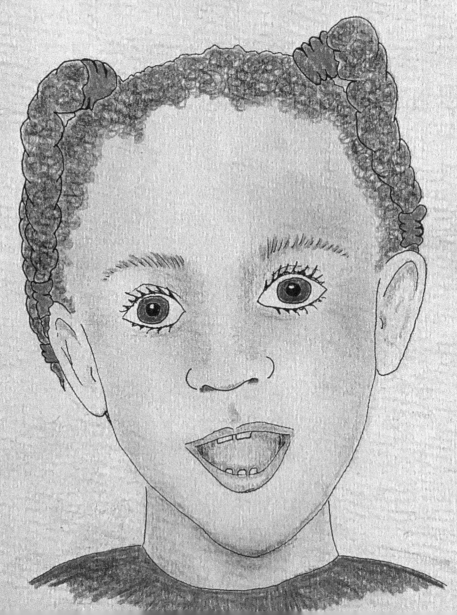

Tick-Tock, Tick-Tock

And now the door is moving too!

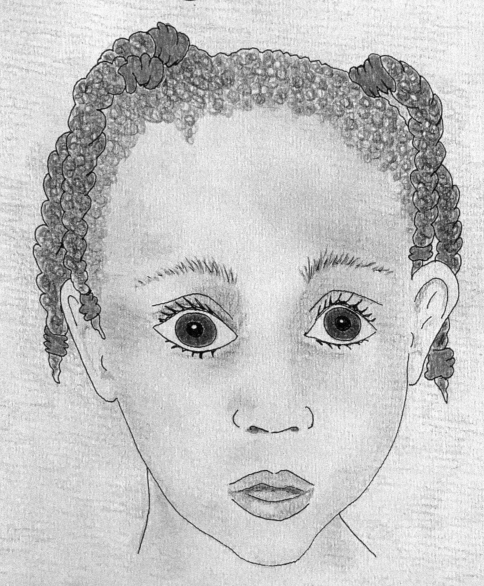

Tick-Tock, Tick-Tock

Cuckoo!
Cuckoo!
Cuckoo!
Cuckoo!

Oh Grandpa!

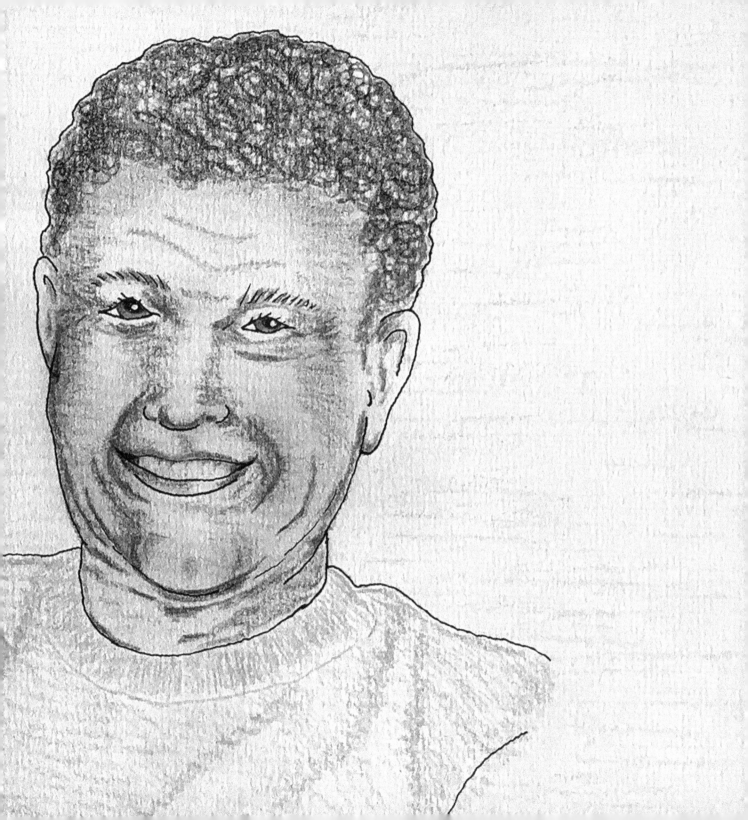

Can you draw a big hand and a little hand to show the time written underneath each clock? I've done the first one for you.

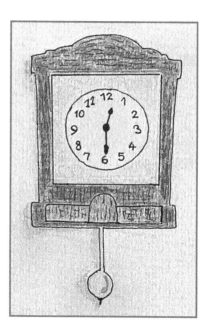

half past 12

7 o'clock

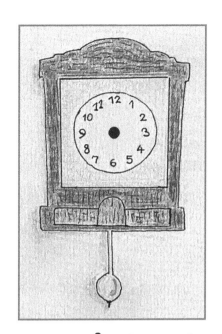

10 o'clock

3 o'clock

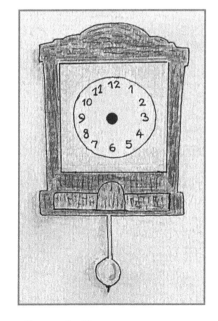

half past 5

quarter to 1

quarter past 4

Why I wrote this book

I hope you enjoyed my story. It's dedicated to my Dad, Stuart Griffiths (aka 'Grandpa') who has always loved to tell stories – and have a good laugh!
When he was a little boy his mum and dad had an old grandfather clock. Every night they made sure that the clock's large, stiff wooden door was firmly shut but each morning they would find the door wide open, as if someone or something had pushed it open.

Creepy! So creepy, in fact, that they eventually got rid of it.

I thought it would be fun to imagine what would happen if a fun-loving grandpa bought a cuckoo clock and then waited to see his granddaughter's reaction when she discovered what was hiding behind its teeny, tiny door.

You can find out more about me and my other stories at tigerseyebooks.co.uk

My other stories

Ready for another grrreat story? Read Tiger Tale

Zarif thinks that he is a very important and scary tiger but will a cat-loving lady feel the same? Find out what happens when the two meet in this rollicking rhyming story.

Watch me read Tiger Tale on my website tigerseyebooks.co.uk

See you... CUCKOO!

Lightning Source UK Ltd.
Milton Keynes UK
UKHW050710080922
408460UK00005B/53

9 781916 194816